To young readers in
Durango, Colorado...
Be smart. Stay safe.
Follow "The RULES!"

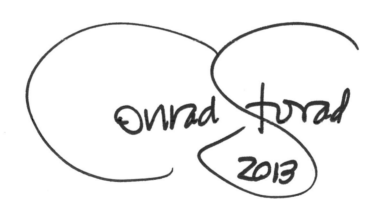

Conrad Storad
2013

RATTLESNAKE RULES

Written by

Conrad J. Storad

Illustrated by

Nathaniel P. Jensen

Linda F. Radke, President
Five Star Publications, Inc.
PO Box 6698
Chandler, AZ 85246-6698
480-940-8182
fax 480-940-8787
www.FiveStarPublications.com
info@FiveStarPublications.com

www.RattlesnakeRules.com

Library of Congress Cataloging-in-Publication Data

Storad, Conrad J.
Rattlesnake rules / by Conrad J. Storad ; illustrated by Nathaniel P.
Jensen. -- 1st ed.
    p. cm.
Summary: A mother rattlesnake who can locate food with her tongue and swallow prey in one gulp shares survival tips with her babies--and with humans.
ISBN 978-1-58985-161-0
[1. Stories in rhyme. 2. Rattlesnakes--Fiction. 3. Snakes--Fiction.] I.
Jensen, Nathaniel P., ill II. Title.
PZ8.3.S8725Rat 2009
[E]--dc22
                        2009027518

Printed in Cananda
10 9 8 7 6 5 4 3 2 1

Manufactured by Friesen's Corporation
Manufactured in Altona, MB, Canada in August 2009
Job #48851

Cover Design and Illustration Design by Nathaniel P. Jensen
Interior Design: Linda Longmire
Project Manager: Sue DeFabis

This Book Belongs To:

_____

Dedication:

To my grandchildren, Bennett, Jacob, Eli, Natalie and Logan.
Learn all about our amazing world. Protect it whenever you can.

- Grandpa Top

Acknowledgments:

Special thanks to editor and friend Paul Howey for casting a keen eye over the manuscript and helping to polish each line to a high sheen. As always, the most heartfelt thank you is for my wife, Laurie. I know you are always there for me each step of the way for every project I pursue. Stay close, we have lots more work to do together.

- Conrad J. Storad
Tempe, Arizona

To Debbie, John, Justin and Zachary
- Nathaniel P. Jensen

RATTLESNAKE RULES

Written by

Conrad J. Storad

Illustrated by

Nathaniel P. Jensen

In deserts and in jungles,
In lakes and in the sea,
Live creatures of all shapes and sizes
That have rules like you and me.

6

Animals learn rules by living.
They have no books or schools.
Please pay attention to this story.
For even rattlesnakes have rules.

Mama Rattler called to her young,
"Gather close. Hear what I *sssay*.
These lessons are important.
There are rules you must obey."

Mama told her babies lots of tales.
She shared tips to keep in mind.
Some were scary, some were fun.
They learned all about their kind.

9

"Rattlesnakes are beautiful," she said.
"We have bodies long and lean.
Our heads look like the Ace of Spades.
We have eyesight that is keen.

10

"Some rattlesnakes have tiger stripes.
Some have diamonds on their backs.
But we all have fangs and venom,
And we all eat mice for snacks."

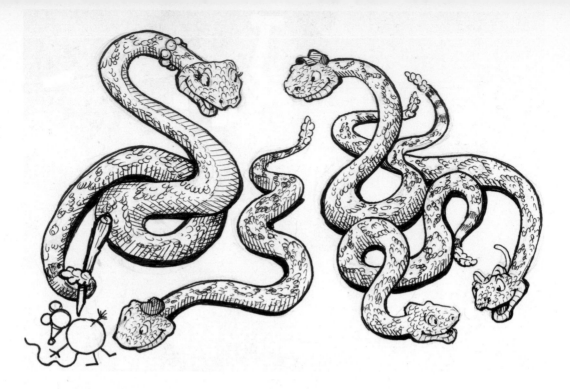

Mama taught them rules for hunting.
She showed them how to play.
She taught her babies rules for eating
To help them survive each day.
"Rattlers hunt both night and day," she said.
"Cool days, warm nights are best.
But when the weather gets really cold,
We coil in our dens to rest."

RULES FOR HUNTING

Rule 1: Flick your forked tongue in and out.

Rule 2: Try not to make a sound.

Your tongue will pick up lots of smells
Both from the air and from the ground.

"Use your pits to locate food.
They can sense a rodent's heat.
Keep flicking until you see the prey.
Then it's almost time to eat.

"Coil tight before you strike," she said.
"Let the prey come near.
WHAM! Strike fast with your fangs;
Your dinnertime is here."

RULES FOR EATING

Rule 1: Open mouth VERY wide!
It's something snakes can do.

Rule 2: Swallow prey in one big gulp!
Rattlers have no teeth with which to chew.

17

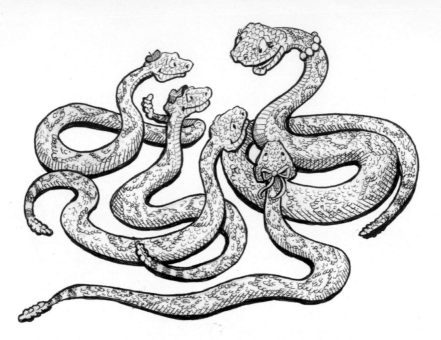

Mama saved the warning rules for last.
The babies pressed close to hear.
She told them when to rattle hard.
She told them things to fear.

As Mama shared her wisdom,
One of her babies began to wail,
"My rattle scares me, Mama.
"I'm afraid of my own tail!"

Mama smiled, then continued,
"Please listen close my dear.
Your rattle makes important sounds.
It makes your message clear."

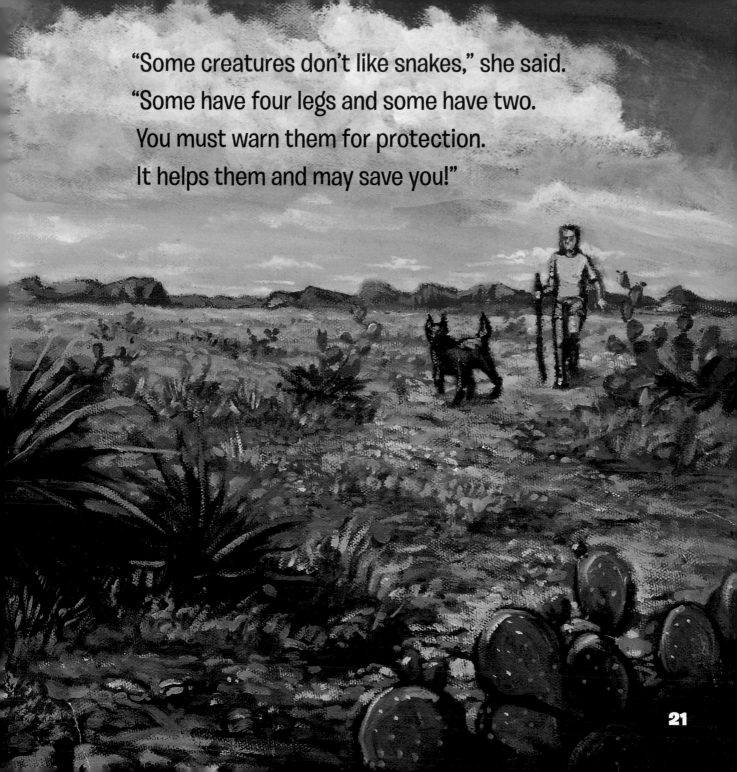

"Some creatures don't like snakes," she said.
"Some have four legs and some have two.
You must warn them for protection.
It helps them and may save you!"

21

RULES OF WARNING

Rule 1: Rattle loud when danger's near.
Shake your rattle without fail.

Rule 2: Rattle even louder.
Don't be scared of your own tail!

Mama Rattler's rules for us are simple.
Just common sense, that's true.
Remember, leave rattlesnakes alone
And they'll never bother you.

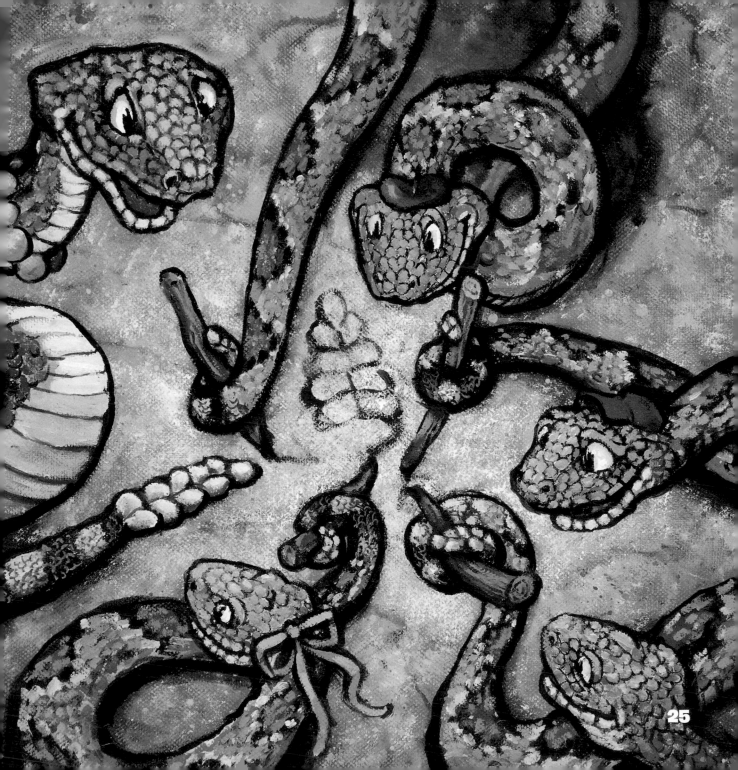

RULES FOR HUMANS

Rule 1: Step back when a snake's tail rattles. This is not a time for fun.

Rule 2: Step back again...*sloooowly.*
A smart move is to **RUN!**

RATTLESNAKE FAST FACTS

Species: More than 30 different species of rattlesnakes are known...so far

Range: Live only in North and South America

Size: 12 inches to 7 feet long; adults can weigh from 1 to 10 pounds

Prey: Rats, mice, other small rodents, squirrels, rabbits, small birds, frogs, toads, lizards, centipedes

Predators: Coyote, fox, bobcat, horned owl, hawk, eagle, King snake

Rattlesnakes are amazing animals, but we still don't know everything there is to know about these creatures. Scientists who study snakes and other reptiles are called herpetologists. They are learning new facts about where rattlesnakes live and how they survive from day to day. There are lots of stories about rattlesnakes. Some are based on facts; some tales are not. As a result, rattlesnakes are creatures of myth and mystery. Want to learn some truths about rattlesnakes? Keep reading. Have fun!

RATTLESNAKE FUN FACTS

Rattlesnakes are pit vipers. The pit organs look like holes located between each eye and the snake's mouth. Rattlers can see well with their eyes during the day. The pit organs help them "see" at night. The pits sense heat. They work kind of like night vision goggles used by soldiers.

A rattlesnake's rattle is made of keratin. Human fingernails, animal horns, and claws are made of the same thing.

A rattlesnake's fangs are like retractable hollow needles.

Arizona has 13 species of rattlesnakes, more than any other state.

Rattlesnakes have glands that make venom. The glands are small sacs that attach to the fangs. We have glands in our mouths that make saliva.

The Eastern Diamondback is the largest rattler of all. These snakes live in the dry pine woods and sandy woodlands of the southeastern United States. Eastern Diamondbacks can grow up to 7 feet long and weigh as much as 10 pounds. They can live for 10 to 20 years in the wild.

The Pygmy rattlesnake is the smallest known rattler. It is usually only about 12 inches long. Pygmy rattlers are found throughout the central and southeastern United States. They live in woods and scrubland and like to hide under piles of leaves and bark litter. Their rattle is tiny.

The Mohave rattlesnake has the most potent venom. It lives in the dry deserts of Arizona, California, Nevada, and in parts of New Mexico, Texas, and Mexico. The Mohave rattler's bite is very dangerous to humans.

RATTLESNAKE MYSTERIES

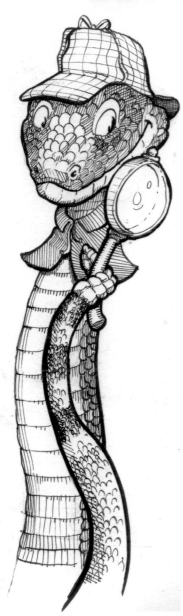

Why did rattlesnakes develop a rattle?

Scientists think that the snake's rattle evolved as a warning device. The noise is a signal or alert. The rattling sound kept large animals from stepping on and crushing the snake. It reminds us to "beware!"

Do rattlesnakes lay eggs?

Most reptiles and many types of snakes do lay eggs. Rattlesnakes are reptiles, but they give birth to live young. The baby snakes develop inside the mother's body until the time of birth.

Do rattlesnakes protect their young?

The young of some kinds of rattlesnakes will stay with their mother until they shed their skin for the first time. This is called molting. The first molt usually happens about two weeks after birth.

How often do rattlesnakes eat?

Rattlesnakes need to catch several meals per month to survive during the warm season when they are most active. But they will eat more often if there is plenty of prey available. The more it eats, the faster and larger a rattlesnake will grow.

RATTLESNAKE MYTHS US. FACTS

Myth: Rattlesnakes add a new rattle each year. By counting the rattles you can tell the age of a rattlesnake.

Truth: Rattlesnakes add a new rattle each time they shed their skin. They can shed many times per year. Rattles can also break off so counting rattles is not a good way to tell a snake's age.

Myth: Rattlesnakes always travel in pairs.

Truth: This is false. However, males and females are often seen together during breeding season (April to June).

Myth: Most rattlesnakes can jump at least two feet.

Truth: Snakes don't have legs. They cannot jump at all! Rattlesnakes can strike a distance of about two-thirds their own body length. It's smart to be cautious and step back slowly when you meet a rattlesnake. Be smart and be safe.

Myth: Rattlesnakes always rattle before striking.

Truth: They may or may not rattle before striking. Watch where you step.

Myth: Rattlesnakes can strike only from a coiled position.

Truth: Rattlesnakes can strike and bite from any position.

Myth: Pull out the fangs of a rattlesnake and you can make it harmless.

Truth: Rattlesnakes can grow new fangs to replace a lost pair.

WORDS TO LEARN

burrow: (BUR-oh) A hole or tunnel dug in the ground. Animals dig burrows to use as a home, nest, or shelter.

glands: Parts of the body that make liquids. Small sac-like glands attached to a rattlesnake's fangs make venom.

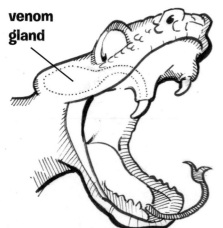

keratin: (KEHR-a-tin) Rough, hard material that forms the segments of a rattlesnake's rattle. It also forms animal hair, horns, claws, and human fingernails.

predator: (PRED-a-tohr) An animal that hunts and eats other animals.

prey: (PRAY) Animals that are hunted and eaten by other animals.

reptiles: Animals whose bodies are covered with scales. Snakes, lizards, alligators, and crocodiles are reptiles.

venom
gland

scales: Small, flat, thickened pieces of skin that cover and protect a snake's body. Different kinds of scales are found on different parts of a rattlesnake.

venom: (VEH-nuhm) Poison. Rattlesnakes inject venom with their fangs when they bite. The venom kills or stuns the prey before it is eaten.

Rattlesnake Rules Curriculum Guide

Sharing books with children can take many forms. A book can just be read aloud or it can be shared through activities. The more interaction the child has with the text, the greater his or her understanding and retention of the material will be. Sharing a book with a child helps create a good reader. A child will see that you value reading and will want to be just like you. Just like learning a new song, the more times a book is read and shared, the more details will be discovered and learned. Each time you read *Rattlesnake Rules*, you can enjoy different activities to help enhance the text.

In order to guide the reading and get the most benefit from the text, follow the three stages of good shared reading. First, do activities to lead the child into the text. Second, keep the child involved during reading. Third, do activities to build on and review what was read and learned. Use all the learning activities: Listening, Speaking, Reading, Writing, and Kinesthetics (movement).

Before Reading Activities

1. Discussion: *What do you already know about snakes? About rattlesnakes?*

2. Word Wall: *Use the glossary at the back of the book to create word strips.* Other words to add are "molting" and "herpetologist." Post the strips on a wall or hand out the strips, one to each child. When the word is used in the story, the child pins the word to the wall and explains the meaning.

3. Chart it: *Create a two-column chart.* At the top of one column put "Predator," and at the top of the other put "Prey." Fill in the columns with animals and their prey. Examples are: bats and mosquitoes, birds and worms, frogs and flies. After reading the book, add snakes and mice.

4. Activity: *Make a rattle*. Use the back of a white paper plate with ridges/fluting around the edge. The edge is the snake's body. Draw the head coiled in on the center flat section and the tail coiled in also in the flat center section. Color it to look like a rattlesnake. Using a second paper plate, place the two plates with their top sides together, and staple or tape them together around the outer edges leaving a small opening. Put some dried beans into the opening and then finish sealing the edge. When it is shaken, it will rattle.

During Reading Activities:

1. Use the rattle that you made and shake it each time the rattlesnake's rattle is mentioned in the story.

2. Snake talk: Every time the word rattlesnake is used in the story, practice snake talk. Say "snake" with several s's (Rattle*sssss*nake) to mimic the sound of the rattle.

3. Using your senses: How do you know your food compared to how a snake knows its food? How does a rattlesnake use its senses compared to how we use ours when we eat? Fill in the chart for the rattlesnake as you read the book. Then add the characteristics of people. Compare the two.

	Rattlesnake	People
Eyes		
Ears		
Nose		
Mouth		
Touch		

Below are the answers from the text, although more can be added after discussion.

	Rattlesnake	People
Eyes	Keen	
Ears	Have no ears	
Nose	Use tongue	
Mouth	Fangs, flick tongue, swallow whole	
Touch	Coil and strike	

4. Safety: Rattlesnakes don't eat people. They don't want to be stepped on either. They often use their rattle to signal their location. What are important rules for people to follow to protect themselves from rattlesnakes? Create a poster like those you see at a swimming pool or in a classroom with rules for people to follow if they hear a rattlesnake.

Answer: **You should have 5 rules**

1. Rattles mean danger, but rattlesnakes don't always rattle a warning.
2. Watch where you walk.
3. Leave rattlesnakes alone.
4. Step away if you hear a rattle.
5. Better yet, run!

After Reading Activities:

1. Snake walk: Lie on the floor and hold your arms close to your sides. Hold your legs and ankles tightly together. Now try to move forward. You will have to bend your hips and knees like a caterpillar or a snake. Try moving sideways. You will have to wiggle half your body at a time like a sidewinder.

2. Molting: Snakes shed their skin, and it comes off inside out. Put a long sock on your arm. Starting near your elbow, peel the sock off of your arm so that it is folding back over itself. Your fingers stay in the sock in the same place until the sock finally comes off of your arm. What does "inside out" mean?

3. Write an acrostic poem about a rattlesnake.

Write the letters S, N, A, K and E on a piece of paper. Use the first letter to begin a thought about snakes. Older children could use R A T T L E S N A K E.

Example:

Snakes slither along the ground
Nice and smooth they go
Always flicking their tongue
Keeping their rules in mind
Every day they look for food

4. Explore: Use the "Fun Facts" and information at the back of the book for further research. Put children in groups to look up more information about one of the facts.

    a. Fact: There are more than 30 species of rattlesnakes.
        Research: Look up the names.
    b. Fact: The Eastern Diamondback is the largest of all.
        Research: Find a picture of this snake.
    c. Fact: Rattlesnakes have no ears. Research: How do they hear?

Conrad Storad's most recent masterpiece, *Rattlesnake Rules*, neatly ties together learning, laughter and love in his tale of a mother and her snakelings. Kids will love the way Conrad entertainingly explains the nature of rattlers in his fun-filled, knowledge-packed story! In addition to being a great read, *Rattlesnake Rules* is truly a useful tool for those seeking to learn about the lives of rattlesnakes. As with all of Conrad's previous titles, parents will enjoy reading this to their children, as much as kids will enjoy hearing it or reading it themselves! *Rattlesnake Rules* will surely bring a smile to any reader's face.

Michael Moorehead

- Michael Moorehead, author of
The Student From Zombie Island: Conquering the Rumor Monster

"Conrad Storad does it again. He continues to bridge the wonder and curiosity of being a child with the importance of education. The author is equally engaging and entertaining as a guest on my radio show. *Rattlesnake Rules* is a must for any classroom and an enjoyable book to share with my own young children. Storad's latest will join his other books in our family collection like *Don't Call Me Pig, Desert Night Shift* and *Lizards for Lunch*. As an advocate for Arizona, and more importantly as a typical parent, I promise that you will love *Rattlesnake Rules*. Coil up and enjoy!"

- Dave Pratt,
Radio Personality and author of *Dave Pratt: Behind the Mic, 30 Years in Radio*

As a mother of five--who happens to live in rattlesnake territory--it's important for me to teach my children to respect the world around them. What better resource for young children than Conrad Storad's latest picture book. *Rattlesnake Rules* provides children with essential lessons about rattlesnakes and their habitat in a fun and engaging way. And Nathaniel Jensen's illustrations are some of the most vibrant I've ever seen!

Because we do encounter rattlesnakes, literally in our own backyard, my kids need to be aware of how these fascinating but potentially deadly creatures behave. From a very young age, they also need to know how to react appropriately if they see one, and I appreciate Conrad Storad's efforts to lay out the ground rules and provide instruction in a nonthreatening way. To stay safe at our house, we have to review the rattlesnake rules every day!"

- Jennifer S. Christensen
Utah Public Radio/Deseret News correspondent

Conrad J. Storad's newest book, *Rattlesnake Rules*, is a highly entertaining and educational window into the world of the much maligned snakes. This book can help change that, for much of our fear about these reptiles has arisen from our ignorance about them. The illustrations by Nathaniel P. Jensen will bring alive the story for young readers and for the adults fortunate enough to read this book to them. I believe children, parents, teachers, and librarians will agree that Conrad, who has a long list of popular educational children's books to his credit, has slugged a home run with *Rattlesnake Rules*.

- Paul M. Howey, award-winning author of
Freckles: The Mystery of the Little White Dog in the Desert

Rattlesnake Rules Order Form

ITEM	QTY	Unit Price	TOTAL
Rattlesnake Rules Signed Copy		$16.95 US $17.95 CAN	
➤➤**Subtotal**			
$8.00 for the first book and $1.00 for each additional book going to the same address. (US rates) **Order 3 or more copies and receive FREE shipping** *Ground shipping only. Allow 1 to 2 weeks for delivery.* ***Shipping**			
➤➤**TOTAL**			

NAME:

ADDRESS:

CITY, STATE, ZIP:

DAYTIME PHONE:　　　　**FAX:**

EMAIL:

Method of Payment:
❑VISA ❑MasterCard ❑Discover Card
❑American Express

account number ▲
_____ / _____ / _____

expiration date ▲

signature ▲

❑ I'm interested in having the author and/or illustrator visit my school. Please contact Linda Radke at 480-940-8182.

❑ Send a Five Star Catalog.

❑ Personalize signed copy.

www.RattlesnakeRules.com

P.O. Box 6698 • Chandler, AZ 85246-6698
(480) 940-8182　866-471-0777　Fax: (480) 940-8787
info@FiveStarPublications.com　www.FiveStarPublications.com

About Little Five Star

Linda Radke, *founder and president of Five Star Publications*

Rattlesnake Rules is published by Little Five Star, a division of Five Star Publications, publishing books exclusively for children.

Our mission is to help authors create books that will help children understand the implications of their life choices and help them become more tolerant and accepting of the differences in people.

www.LittleFiveStar.com